COLLEGE LIBRARY

**Please return this book by the date stamped below
- if recalled, the loan is reduced to 10 days**

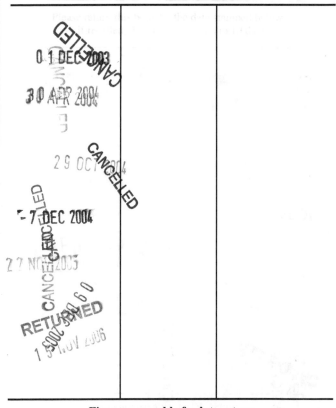
Fines are payable for late return

PUFFIN BOOKS

THE VANISHMENT OF THOMAS TULL

When Thomas Tull was seven years old he stopped growing, which was bad, and began shrinking, which was worse. His parents were very upset and began to seek ways to restore their much-loved son to his former size.

A French chef, three doctors, the Double-Sighted Youth, a duchess, a flying ace baron and countless others all tried their personal, patent cures for this mysterious shrinking ailment – which involved young Thomas in some hair-raising adventures!

This wonderfully zany story has been created by the best-selling team of Janet and Allan Ahlberg, whose previous books include *Peepo!*, *The Baby's Catalogue* (both Picture Puffins), the *Happy Families* series and *The Ha Ha Bonk Book*. Janet and Allan Ahlberg both trained as teachers in Sunderland College of Education, where they met. Janet went on to study graphic design and became an illustrator. Allan has had a variety of occupations, including postman, grave-digger, soldier, plumber's mate, school teacher, headmaster, and is now a full-time writer ('the best job I have so far come upon'). Today they are bestsellers with numerous titles in print for several different publishers.

THE VANISHMENT OF THOMAS TULL

Janet and Allan Ahlberg

Puffin Books

PUFFIN BOOKS

Published by the Penguin Group
27 Wrights Lane, London W8 5TZ, England
Viking Penguin Inc., 40 West 23rd Street, New York, New York 10010, USA
Penguin Books Australia Ltd, Ringwood, Victoria, Australia
Penguin Books Canada Ltd, 2801 John Street, Markham, Ontario, Canada L3R 1B4
Penguin Books (NZ) Ltd, 182–190 Wairau Road, Auckland 10, New Zealand

Penguin Books Ltd, Registered Offices: Harmondsworth, Middlesex, England

First published by A. & C. Black Ltd 1977
Published in Puffin Books 1985
7 9 10 8 6

Copyright © Janet and Allan Ahlberg, 1977
All rights reserved

Made and printed in Great Britain by
Richard Clay Ltd, Bungay, Suffolk
Filmset in Monophoto Times

When Thomas Tull was seven years old he stopped growing, which was bad, and began shrinking, which was worse. By the time he was seven and a half none of his clothes fitted him at all; and when his eighth birthday arrived he had to stand on a box to blow his candles out.

Mr and Mrs Tull were much upset by the slow disappearance of their son. In the beginning Mrs Tull said, 'That boy just needs to eat more. Eating makes you grow, it is a proven fact!'

'Yes dear,' said Mr Tull, and he went out to find a chef.

✺✺✺

The chef's name was Monsieur Alphonse and he was the best chef in the whole of France. Although he spoke no English, Monsieur Alphonse managed to make his wishes known. He wanted two cooks and a wine waiter to help him, and insisted that the kitchen be enlarged. When everything was to his satisfaction Monsieur Alphonse set to work.

Soon the Tulls' house was full of the smell of marvellous cooking and the Tulls' dining-table was piled high with all kinds of beautiful and delicious food: roast ribs of beef and potato pasties; pigeon pie and turkey cooked in wine; fresh hearts of celery in lobster sauce; Bologna sausages; Swiss buns and sweetbreads; Indian fritters, brandy balls and cream; Royal Coburg pudding and Folkestone pudding pies; rum butter and apple marmalade tart; chocolate neapolitan fudge; melons and nectarines; muffins and tea; toast and various imported jams.

Monsieur Alphonse sets to work

But the cooking of Monsieur Alphonse did no good. Each night, no matter what he had eaten during the day, Thomas Tull weighed just a little *less* than he had weighed the night before. The other members of the Tull family put on weight but that, of course, was not the idea.

After a while Monsieur Alphonse went back to France, the cooks and the wine waiter went away also, and Mrs Tull said, 'Chefs are not the answer. What that boy needs is medical attention!'

'Yes dear,' said Mr Tull, and he went out to find a doctor.

Mr Tull found three doctors altogether; Doctor Groper of Amsterdam, Doctor Gristlebone of Boston and the Honourable Doctor Chop-Chop of China.

When Doctor Groper had examined Thomas Tull from top to toe he said, 'Vat dis liddel chap vant is plenty pill, injection und such tinks like dis.' And he set to work.

When Doctor Gristlebone had examined Thomas Tull with stethoscopes and microscopes,

X-ray machines and little wooden hammers he said, 'I reckon I will hang and stretch this boy for a while and see what happens.' Soon Doctor Gristlebone was drilling a large number of holes in the walls, floor and ceiling of the Tulls' spare bedroom in order to screw down, or up, the various contraptions he had brought with him and was planning to use.

When the Honourable Doctor Chop-Chop had examined Thomas Tull using a feather and a rolled-up newspaper, he didn't say anything. He simply took Thomas away to his laboratory and put him in an enormous machine. This machine was called the Enlargero-Phonotron and was the only one of its kind in the whole world.

But the Honourable Doctor Chop-Chop's Enlargero-Phonotron did no good. Thomas Tull didn't get bigger, he got smaller. The Honourable Doctor Chop-Chop's pet rabbit got bigger, but that was an accident. Somehow she hopped into the Enlargero-Phonotron when no one was looking and by the time the Doctor let her out it was too late.

Doctor Groper's pills and powders, embrocations and healing ointments, stimulating injections

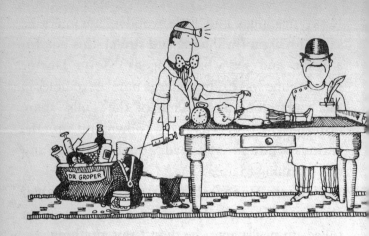

and soothing herbal wines, also did no good. Each time Thomas put his tongue out to say 'Ah!' it was obvious to all that, though the tongue itself was pink and healthy, its size was dwindling.

Doctor Gristlebone's stretching and hanging contraptions did no good either. Thomas Tull didn't get longer, he got shorter. When at last Doctor Gristlebone, in exasperation, tightened one of his contraptions beyond the safe limits for its use, all that happened was the floor fell in and Doctor Gristlebone himself dropped through into the room below. Luckily for Doctor Gristlebone, he landed on Mr and Mrs Tull's bed. Luckily for Mr and Mrs Tull, they were not in it at the time.

After a while the three doctors handed in their bills to Mr Tull and went away.

Thomas was eight now and standing on a box to blow his birthday candles out. By the time he was eight and a half he was no bigger than his little sister who was three; and when his ninth birthday arrived he was smaller than the cat.

As the months went by, Thomas Tull had trouble with the cat who began to look at him in a puzzled way and jump out and chase him when no one was about. He had trouble also with the next-door neighbour's dog and with his own one-time little, but now big, sister. This sister's name was Annabelle, and it was her delight to dress Thomas

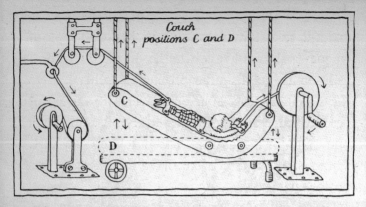

Couch positions C and D

Neck Stretcher

Finger Stretcher

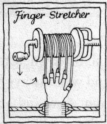

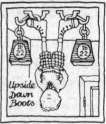

Upside Down Boots

Adjustable Weights

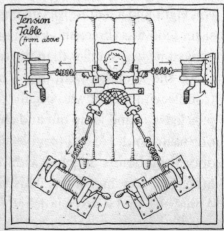

Tension Table (from above)

Doctor Gristlebone's contraptions

up and take him for walks in her doll's pram whenever she could and whether he liked it or not.

Thomas had a similar problem at school. Here the girls in his class quarrelled over who should sit next to him, who should carry his books and which one of them it was that Thomas liked the best. Thomas said he didn't like any of them, but he was not believed.

'Who will you marry when you grow up, Thomas?' the girls said.

'Nobody,' said Thomas. 'And anyway, I'm not growing up – I'm growing down!'

Now once a month Mr Tull weighed and measured his son and wrote up the results in a special notebook. Partly this was to help Mrs Tull with the increasingly difficult job of finding new clothes for Thomas. The other reason, of course, was to see just exactly how bad things were getting. When Thomas was nine and a half Mr Tull wrote:

Weight	*23 pounds*
Height	*1 foot 1$\frac{1}{2}$ inches*
Chest	*7 inches*
Length of leg	*6 inches*
Length of arm	*4$\frac{3}{4}$ inches*
Length of little finger	*$\frac{3}{8}$ of an inch*

'Goodness me,' said Mrs Tull. 'Length of little finger three eighths of an inch – that is a disaster!'

'Yes dear,' said Mr Tull.

'We mothers don't have babies just to watch them melt away, you know!'

'No dear,' said Mr Tull.

'Well, do something!' said Mrs Tull. 'Advertise – offer a reward – that should do the trick!'

'Yes dear,' said Mr Tull, and he went out to find a printer.

ᘺᘺᘺ

The posters which the printer made were put up all over the town, and they said:

£1000 REWARD
One thousand pounds reward is offered
to any man, woman or child
who is able to prevent
MASTER THOMAS TULL
of 158 BALACLAVA ROAD
from shrinking away.
A further one thousand pounds
will be paid to anyone who can restore
this well-loved but unfortunate boy
to his former size.

During the next six months, four hundred and
eighty-nine men, women and children came to the
Tulls' house; also two parrots, one performing seal
and a dwarf.

Grandma Bottler forgetting about Thomas

All these visitors experimented on Thomas Tull in various ways. Some gave him things to eat; some gave him things to drink; a few made him do exercises and stand on his head; and one small girl tried to inflate him with a bicycle pump, before her mother saw what she was doing and gave her a smack.

A man who called himself 'The Irresistible Rollo' tried – without success – to hypnotize Thomas; an old lady named Grandma 'Gipsy' Bottler arranged for him to stand in a bowl of special water by the light of the full moon, and then went off and forgot all about him; and a retired medicine man of the Apache Indians, now touring as a drummer with the Buffalo Buckskin Band, was stopped from giving him a pipe to smoke by Mrs Tull. She wasn't having any son of hers smoking pipes at the age of nine and three quarters, she said, no matter what!

The parrots, who were brought to the house by their owner, said supposedly magic words; the seal made supposedly magic movements with its flippers, and the dwarf tried to persuade Thomas to 'think big'. When Thomas asked the dwarf why he hadn't tried this on himself, the dwarf said, 'Oh,

but I have! Before thinking big I was the *littlest* thing you ever saw.'

The last visitors to see Thomas Tull were Captain Warren and his son the Double-Sighted Youth. The Double-Sighted Youth had a silk scarf tied over his eyes and answered questions about the future. When he was asked about Thomas Tull he said, 'This boy, before the year is out, will fly with a baron, dance with a duchess and shake hands with the King.'

'I don't want to dance with a duchess,' said Thomas Tull.

'Don't be so ungrateful, Thomas,' said his mother. Then to the Double-Sighted Youth she said, 'What else?'

'He will disappear,' said the Youth.

'Aaaargh!' said Mrs Tull and she fainted away on the floor.

Mr Tull knelt down beside his wife and gave her a glass of water. Looking up at the Youth he said, 'Is that all?'

'That is all,' said the Youth.

After which his father said, 'Not quite er ... twenty-five pounds please.'

〽〽〽

When his tenth birthday arrived Thomas Tull was so small he had to stand on the *cake* to blow his candles out.

One of his birthday presents was a toy fort complete with half a dozen matchstick-firing cannons and a set of soldiers. Soon Thomas began living in the fort. His father made a small bed for him which fitted into it and Thomas felt comfortable in the company of the soldiers who were all just that bit smaller than he was.

From now on Thomas Tull no longer went to school and his sister Annabelle was told not to dress him up any more for fear that she might accidentally squash him. Also the Tulls' cat was sent away to stay with Thomas's grandma in another town. But with the cat gone, the birds began to take an interest in Thomas. After all, some of them were accustomed to eat creatures of his size by the beakful. Spiders too were a problem for him, and when it rained in the garden Thomas frequently had to swim back to the house.

Thomas was now the smallest person that had ever lived and he was becoming famous for it. His photograph and measurements appeared in all the newspapers. The Mayor of the town made a speech about him. The Duchess of Old Hill arranged a grand ball in his honour.

As predicted by the Double-Sighted Youth, the Duchess danced with Thomas at the ball. She did this with the help of a special contraption the Duke

Problems for Thomas

had had made for her, and in spite of all Thomas's efforts to get away.

Shortly after this Thomas was called to Buckingham Palace to shake hands, not just with the King, but with the entire Royal Family.

Then, on the very evening of Thomas's return from the Palace, the Baron von Bolivar, famous flying-ace and dare-devil extraordinary, landed his single-seater de Havilland biplane in the Tulls' garden. The Baron enjoyed being famous and was always looking for things to do which would make him more famous. Now he had the idea that

Thomas Tull should fly with him to Rome and then to Paris.

'It vill be ze most *famous* thing!' he said.

Mr and Mrs Tull looked closely at the biplane. Already a tiny cockpit had been added for Thomas to sit in.

'It vill be a triumph!' said the Baron.

'Will it be safe, though?' said Mrs Tull.

'It vill be glorious!' said the Baron. 'Zis I know! All ze peoples vill cheer und throw zer 'ats in ze air – zis I know! But "safe"? Zis I don't know.'

In spite of this Mr and Mrs Tull agreed that Thomas could go. As Mrs Tull said, he wasn't getting any bigger, sitting round the house; maybe the change of air would do him good. The next morning, therefore, Thomas Tull put on his overcoat and a warm woolly hat, packed a few things in a little bag and flew off with the Baron von Bolivar to Rome.

\WWW/

In Rome all the people cheered and threw their hats in the air; the Baron received a medal and a kiss on each cheek from the Prime Minister of

Italy, and Thomas was presented with a hand-embroidered miniature silk parachute by an admirer of the Baron's. He was also offered a number of pills and herbal lozenges by Doctor Groper, who happened to be in Rome at the time. Most of these, however, were too big for Thomas to carry, let alone swallow, and while the Doctor was arranging for them to be ground up into powders, the Baron's de Havilland biplane was already taxiing along the runway.

'To Paris!' shouted the Baron. 'Arrivederci Roma!' He waved to the Prime Minister and blew kisses to certain ladies in the crowd.

As they were taking off, Thomas Tull said, 'Will all the people cheer in Paris also?'

'All of zem,' said the Baron. He was still blowing kisses over the side of the biplane. 'Every von!'

In Paris all the people cheered and quite a few sang patriotic songs. The Baron received a medal and a kiss on each cheek from the Prime Minister of France; Thomas was presented with a miniature flying helmet by another admirer of the Baron's, and the best chef in all France – Monsieur Alphonse – produced the finest feast of his career, out there on the runway.

On his return from Paris, Thomas Tull parachuted down into the garden where his parents and his sister Annabelle were waiting for him. Overhead the Baron von Bolivar looped the loop for a little while and then flew low over the garden, blowing kisses to the lady next door and shouting out as he went by, 'Arrivederci Thomas Tull! It vas a *famous* thing – zis I know!'

That evening Mr Tull weighed and measured his son and wrote up the results as usual in the special notebook. It was soon clear that neither the change of air nor the renewed acquaintance with

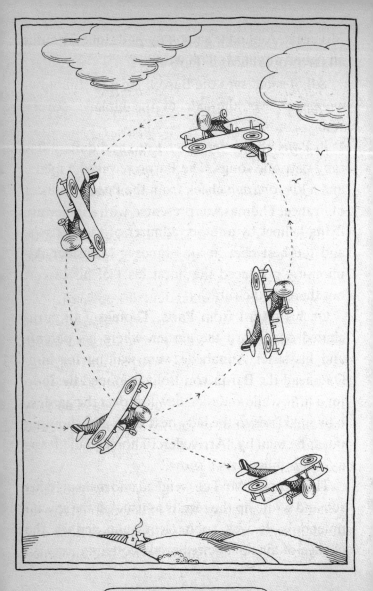

Looping the loop

Monsieur Alphonse's cooking had done Thomas any good at all. Mr Tull wrote:

Weight	*5½ ounces*
Height	*3 inches*
Chest	*1½ inches*
Length of leg	*1¼ inches*
Length of arm	*1 inch*
Length of little finger	*$\frac{3}{32}$ of an inch*

'Bless my soul,' said Mrs Tull. 'Length of little finger three thirty-secondths of an inch – Ernest, we are going to lose that boy!'

Two days later Thomas Tull disappeared.

At the same time the entire contents of all the downstairs rooms in the Tulls' house also disappeared: furniture and clocks, carpets and curtains, cat basket and lampshades, tablecloths and doormat, potted plants – everything. Thomas Tull's toy fort had been in one of the downstairs rooms, and that had gone. Thomas Tull had been in the fort and therefore he had gone as well.

When Mrs Tull got up to make the breakfast that morning and saw what had happened she sat down in the middle of the sitting-room floor and screamed. When Mr Tull saw what had happened

he phoned for the police. And when the police saw what had happened they said, 'Burglars!'

'Burglars!' shouted Mrs Tull. 'Burglars – kidnappers! They've got my little boy!'

'Yes,' said Annabelle. 'All five and a half ounces of him.'

✠✠✠

The burglars, of course, did have Thomas Tull,

although they didn't know they had him – not yet.

What had happened was this: in the dark early hours of the morning, when all the Tulls were fast asleep, a gang of burglars known as the Baggeridge Brothers had broken into the house and stolen everything in sight. The Baggeridge Brothers were five bad men and a boy, and he was bad also – some said he was worse. Their names were Walter, Percy, Sid, Oliver, Albert and

George. George was the boy; it was he who had taken the fort.

The brothers had a large van painted to look like an ambulance. Into this van they loaded the Tulls' property and the Tulls' only son and sped off through the silent streets. Thomas Tull and his toy fort were in a sack with a lot of other things, bouncing about on the floor of the van. Thomas, still tucked up in his little bed, was trying to work out what was going on.

At last the van pulled up outside the Baggeridge Brothers' hideout. Thomas felt himself being lifted up and carried on someone's shoulder along a corridor, perhaps, and then up several flights of stairs. There was a bump as the sack was lowered to the floor. A light went on and through the thin material of the sack Thomas could see dim figures moving.

After a time he heard voices and a sound like sausages sizzling in a pan. It was sausages sizzling in a pan – actually, it was the Tulls' sausages sizzling in the Tulls' pan. Thomas could smell them, and beans also, and tea and cigarettes and beer. Later on Thomas heard the 'clump, clump!' of heavy boots being dropped to the floor and a

30

The Baggeridge Brothers

chorus of voices calling out, ''Night George, 'Night Walter, 'Night Sid, 'Night Percy, 'Night Oliver, 'Night Albert!' After which the light went out and there was a period of silence, followed by snoring.

Thomas found a small hole in the sack and crept out. Ragged curtains were drawn across the windows but enough of the early morning sunlight was getting into the room for him to see where he was.

It was a huge room full of stolen property – the Tulls' and other people's. There was a sink piled high with dirty washing-up. There was a cat basket

– the Tulls' cat basket – with a giant ginger cat sleeping in it. There were a good many pairs of boots and trousers, odd socks and shirts, underpants and vests scattered over the floor. And there were six beds – three pairs of bunk beds, that is – with sleeping burglars in them.

Thomas looked for a door and, when he saw one, began to creep towards it. He wasn't too worried about waking the Baggeridge Brothers – by the sound of things they'd sleep for hours; but he was worried about waking the cat. At the bottom of the door there was a gap. Thomas crouched down, crawled through and found himself in another room. This room was empty except for a large trunk in the middle of the floor, a small iron bed in one corner and a young man with a silk scarf tied over his eyes sitting on the bed and handcuffed, or rather feetcuffed, to it by his ankles.

It was the Double-Sighted Youth.

Thomas was surprised to meet the Youth in such a place at such a time. The Youth, however, even with the scarf over his eyes, was not surprised to meet Thomas. But then, of course, he was double-sighted.

'What are you doing here?' said Thomas.

'It was an accident,' said the Youth. 'My father, Captain Warren, sometimes asks me to hide in a trunk when we are travelling. It is cheaper. Unfortunately, on this occasion the Baggeridge Brothers stole the trunk and me with it.'

'Didn't you know it was going to happen, though?' said Thomas. 'Didn't you look into the future?'

'Yes,' said the Youth. 'Unfortunately, on this occasion I got the date wrong. That happens sometimes.'

Thomas and the Double-Sighted Youth now

Travelling cheaper

made plans for their escape. The Youth told Thomas that all the doors were locked and double-bolted; that the keys were under Walter Bagger-idge's pillow on an upper bunk, and that the bottom of the stairs was guarded by a small but very bad-tempered dog.

'So this is what we do,' said the Youth. 'You go back into the other room and look for a reel of fishing line which you will find under George Baggeridge's bed – he's the littlest of them. You tie the reel itself to a leg of the bed and the loose end of the line around your own waist.'

'Then what?' said Thomas.

'Then you climb up the left hand yellow cur-tain,' said the Youth, 'until you reach a windowpane – the second on the right – in which the glass has been replaced by a piece of cardboard. You push the cardboard aside, climb out and lower yourself to the ground.'

'Right,' said Thomas. 'How high up is it?'

'Five floors,' said the Youth. 'When you reach the ground you fetch the police and they surround the house. After a rumpus and a certain amount of chasing around, and hiding under beds and floorboards and such like, the Baggeridge Brothers get caught, locked up and sent for trial.'

'Good,' said Thomas. He set off for the door.

'The bad-tempered dog and the ginger cat get caught also,' said the Youth; 'you and I have our photographs in the newspapers, and your parents invite me and my father to dinner, three days from now.'

'That's nice,' said Thomas. 'What will we eat?'

'Roast duck,' said the Youth.

'My favourite,' said Thomas and he disappeared under the door.

From then on, everything that the Double-Sighted Youth had said would happen, did happen. The Baggeridge Brothers were surrounded, chased and captured; the bad-tempered dog was carried away in a net, and Thomas Tull and the Double-Sighted Youth were photographed for the newspapers. Only the ginger cat spoilt things when, following a fierce battle with a number of policemen, policewomen and police dogs, it somehow managed to scramble up on to the roof and get away.

Nor was it ever seen again.

Three days later Mr and Mrs Tull, Thomas Tull and Annabelle sat in the dining-room of their house eating roast duck with Captain Warren and the Double-Sighted Youth. When the meal was over, Mrs Tull talked to the Double-Sighted Youth about his powers.

'Can you see everything in the future?' she said.

The rumpus

'No,' said the Youth. 'Sometimes I see a few days very clearly; sometimes I just see one or two things a long way off.'

'And sometimes he gets the date wrong,' said Thomas.

'What about my brother?' said Annabelle. 'What can you see about him?'

'He will go on a journey,' said the Youth.

'I've just been on a journey,' said Thomas.

'He will have trouble with a crocodile,' said the Youth.

'Aaaargh!' said Mrs Tull and she fainted and slumped back in her chair.

'He will smoke a pipe with a medicine man of the Apache Indians,' said the Youth.

Mr Tull leaned over to his wife and gave her a glass of water. 'Is that all?' he said.

'No,' said the Youth. 'One more thing – he will grow.'

The medicine man, of course, was the same medicine man who had come to see Thomas Tull nearly ten months ago. Since then, however, he had left the country. The Buffalo Buckskin Band had continued its world tour and was now in Africa, somewhere between Zanzibar and Bulawayo, it was believed, and heading south.

This news was naturally disturbing to the Tulls, although Mr Tull, at least, did not despair. While Mrs Tull was telling Annabelle and Thomas what a big place Africa was, and Annabelle was telling Mrs Tull and Thomas how jam-packed with crocodiles its rivers were, Mr Tull found out where Baron von Bolivar was staying and talked to him over the telephone.

'Thomas has to go to Africa to see a medicine man,' said Mr Tull.

'Ah,' said the Baron. 'Und you vish 'im to fly?'

'It would help,' said Mr Tull. 'You see, there isn't much time.'

'Vill it be a famous thing?' said the Baron.

'Absolutely,' said Mr Tull.

There was a pause.

'OK,' said the Baron. 'I pack some thing in a bag, drink a little glass beer und fly into your garden in ... four hour. Arrivederci!'

So it was that in the early hours of the following

morning Thomas Tull – by this time less than three inches tall and weighing only five and a quarter ounces – flew off to Africa with the Baron von Bolivar.

In the next few weeks Thomas and the Baron had many adventures. They travelled not only by aeroplane but also by train, steamboat, camel, horse, elephant, ostrich, ox cart, motor bike and balloon. They had trouble with red ants and man-eating orchids and were, at various times, attacked by hippopotamuses, vultures, wild pigs, blood-sucking bats, bandits, crocodiles, giant bees and a lady butterfly collector. This lady mistook Thomas

for a rare specimen of grub and thought the Baron was trying to steal him away.

At last, however, Thomas and the Baron caught up with the medicine man in the South African town of Mafeking. The Buffalo Buckskin Band was just finishing a matinee performance in the town hall gardens. As soon as the final applause had died away and the audience dispersed, the Baron stepped up on to the stage. When the medicine man saw the Baron he came out from behind his drums, shook hands with him and asked him for his autograph. When he saw Thomas Tull he said, 'Howdy, Thomas Tull, is that you?'

Adventures in Africa

'Yes,' said Thomas. He was sitting up in the pocket of the Baron's shirt.

'Shucks, you is truly all shrunk up, ain't you?' said the medicine man.

'Yes,' said Thomas.

'Makes no matter,' said the medicine man. He fumbled in a leather bag hanging at his waist and took out a small pipe.

'See now, I'm gonna fat you up, real good!'

The medicine man pushed some dried leaves and little flowers into the bowl of the pipe and set light to them with a match. Then he held the pipe out to Thomas and said, 'Take a puff.'

Thomas puffed on the pipe with some difficulty. He was not used to smoking, and besides, the pipe was so much bigger than he was.

'Puff some more,' said the medicine man. Thomas did so.

When he had been smoking for about fifteen minutes the medicine man said, 'Now, how you feel?'

Thomas coughed a little and wiped some tears from his eyes. Then he looked at himself and measured his hand against the pattern on the Baron's shirt.

'I feel . . . bigger!' he said.

〰〰〰

From the moment that he began smoking the medicine man's pipe Thomas Tull stopped shrinking, which was good, and began growing, which was better. As an added advantage, the rate at

which he grew was much faster than the rate at which he had shrunk. After only one week he was as big as a new-born baby, and by the end of a fortnight he was the size he used to be when he was seven.

What the leaves and little flowers were that caused this sudden growth, the medicine man refused to say. His only comment was that they

Thomas's return

were 'good-good stuff' his poppa showed him; just one of the range of treatments even a retired medicine man would know about, if he was an Apache, that is.

Now here, strictly speaking, we have reached the end of the story of the vanishment of Thomas Tull. After all, Thomas wasn't vanishing any more, he was growing.

However ...

One week later, at about three o'clock in the afternoon, two parachutists landed in the Tulls' garden. One of them was Thomas Tull now fully restored to his proper size, if anything he was slightly bigger than he should be. The other was the medicine man, come to collect his reward. Overhead the Baron von Bolivar looped the loop for a little while in his Curtis flying-boat and then flew off in the direction of South America, which was a place he had often thought it would be famous to fly to.

Back in the garden Thomas and the medicine man were soon joined by the delighted members of Thomas's family. Thomas was hugged and kissed and told how big he'd grown, and the medicine man was shaken hands with – especially by Annabelle. After this the medicine man received his money and the warm thanks of Mr and Mrs Tull, and went away. The Tulls, meanwhile, had decided to celebrate. This they did by eating ice-cream in the Italian ice-cream shop, buying clothes for Thomas at the best boys' outfitters in the town and seeing Charlie Chaplin in *The Gold Rush* at the Roxy.

Later that evening, when the children were in bed, Mr and Mrs Tull sat by the fire in the sitting-room. Mrs Tull had begun knitting a cardigan for Thomas and Mr Tull, with a long-handled fork in his hand, was toasting tea-cakes.

'You know, Ernest,' said Mrs Tull, 'somebody should write a book about all this.'

'Yes dear,' said Mr Tull.

'I don't suppose anybody would believe it, though.'

'No dear,' said Mr Tull.

'Still, it would have a happy ending,' said Mrs Tull. 'That's the main thing.'

The next morning Thomas and his sister Annabelle went off to school and Mrs Tull wrote a letter to Thomas's grandma telling her the good news and arranging for the return of the Tulls' cat. During the day, as she dusted round the house and did some weeding in the garden, Mrs Tull sang a little song to herself of her own composing. It went like this:

All's well, trala trala,
Trala, trala, trala!

Unfortunately, when Thomas came home from school that afternoon, there were signs that all was not well. He was walking in his stockinged-feet because his shoes, he said, had got too small for him. That evening, over dinner, one of Thomas's shirt-buttons popped off and landed in his mother's soup; and when bedtime came he had to borrow a pair of his father's pyjamas because his own just didn't fit him any more.

The trouble was, of course, Thomas was still growing. Moreover, having reached his present size in only a few weeks, he was, as his sister Annabelle said, now shooting up like a bean-stalk. Soon he had to live in a bell tent at the bottom of the garden because he couldn't get into the house. He became famous once more, this time as the Biggest Boy in the World, and when his eleventh birthday arrived it took twenty-four cooks to make his cake and two lorries to deliver it.

On the day before Thomas's birthday, Mr Tull – with some help from the local fire brigade – weighed and measured his son and wrote up the

The birthday cake

results in the special notebook. Mr Tull wrote:

Weight	*532 pounds*
Height	*19 feet 8$\frac{1}{2}$ inches*
Chest	*10 feet 1 inch*
Length of leg	*9 feet 3 inches*
Length of arm	*7 feet 11 inches*
Length of little finger	*8$\frac{3}{4}$ inches*

'Oh, Ernest,' said Mrs Tull, 'height nineteen feet eight and a half inches – this is no happy ending, is it?'

'No dear,' said Mr Tull.

'That boy's just going up and down like a yoyo!'

'Yes dear,' said Mr Tull.

'Makes me wonder,' said Mrs Tull, 'what in the world can happen next!'

Well, what happened next – and by all accounts a good deal did happen, involving Captain Warren and the Double-Sighted Youth again,

Doctor Chop-Chop, Grandma 'Gipsy' Bottler and many others – what happened next is really another story. Not 'The Vanishment of Thomas Tull' this time, but rather 'The Rapid and Tremendous Growth of Thomas Tull'. It is an interesting story, I believe. Certainly Mrs Tull thinks so. In her opinion someone should write a book about it.

HAPPY FAMILIES

A series of twelve easy-to-read books based on the traditional Happy Families card game. Each story has been written by Allan Ahlberg and uses real-life vocabulary with plenty of humour to describe entertaining events from the life of a different family. The colourfully detailed illustrations and broad interest level of the stories makes them ideal for learner-readers from age five upwards.

THE HA HA BONK BOOK

A book full of jokes to tell your dad, your mum, your baby brother, your teacher and anybody else you can think of. (*Young Puffin*)

THE BABY'S CATALOGUE

A friendly, funny book looking at a day – and a night – in five families. It shows a vast array of baby paraphernalia that will be instantly recognizable to a baby or young child. (*Picture Puffin*)

PEEPO!

With an ingenious hole on every spread to peek through, here's a picture book with a gentle nostalgic flavour. (*Picture Puffin*)

THE OLD JOKE BOOK

Question: What should you do if you like to groan, laugh, shriek and giggle?
Answer: Read *The Old Joke Book* – you'll love it, if you can stand it! (*Picture Puffin*)

RAGDOLLY ANNA
Jean Kenward

Although she's only made from a morsel of this and a tatter of that, Ragdolly Anna is a very special doll. And within hours of beginning to live with the Little Dressmaker, the White Cat and Dummy, she embarks on some hair-raising adventures. Six delightful stories for children of five to seven.

LITTLE DOG LOST
Nina Warner Hooke

Pepito is a bright-eyed, cheerful little dog, with ears too big for his head and a funny short tail. He was born in an old cardboard box in a corner of a Spanish fruit market but one fateful day he is separated from his mother and from then on he seems destined for travel and adventure. But will he ever find what he so yearns for – a *real* home?

THE RAILWAY CAT
Phyllis Arkle

Alfie the railway cat lives at the station where he's a favourite with all the regular passengers. The only trouble is that Hack, the new Railway Porter, doesn't like cats and he soon has a plan for getting rid of Alfie.

DRAGONRISE
Kathryn Cave

When the dragon Tom found under his bed told him what dragons like to eat best, Tom began to worry. He tried to offer his new friend all sorts of tasty morsels as a substitute, but the dragon just wasn't interested. Then Tom's elder sister Sarah did something he couldn't forgive, and he realized that the dragon could help him to take a very unusual revenge!

THE DEAD LETTER BOX
Jan Mark

Louie got the idea from an old film which showed how spies left their letters in a secret place – a dead letter box. It was just the kind of thing that she and Glenda needed to help them keep in touch. And she knew the perfect place for it!

DINNER LADIES DON'T COUNT
Bernard Ashley

Two children, two problems and trouble at school These two stories show that when things can't possibly get worse, help comes in surprising ways.

DUCK BOY
Christobel Mattingley

The holiday at Mrs Perry's farm doesn't start very well for Adam. His older brother and sister don't want to spend any time with him, so he's bored and lonely. But then he discovers the creek and meets two old ducks who obviously need some help. Every year their eggs are stolen by rats or foxes, so Adam strikes a bargain with them: he'll help guard their nest, they'll let him learn to swim in their creek.

THE TALES OF OLGA DA POLGA
Michael Bond

The first collection of tall tales from the guinea-pig with extraordinary gifts, but with a lot of practical advice on how to keep guinea-pigs healthy and happy.

THE PERFECT HAMBURGER
Alexander McCall Smith

If only Joe could remember *exactly* what he had thrown so haphazardly into the mixing bowl, he knew that his perfect hamburger could revive his friend Mr Borthwick's ailing business and drive every other fast-food store off the high street.

SUN AND RAIN
Ann Ruffell

It hasn't rained for seven weeks. The Smallwood family have had enough, and are sending off for all sorts of heat-wave 'special offers'. First to arrive is Susan's rain-making kit, and soon a rain cloud appears in the spotless blue sky – one solitary cloud which is fixed firmly over the Smallwoods' house!

THE HICCUPS AT NO. 13
Gyles Brandreth

The Brown family are looking forward to a relaxing Sunday morning but when Hamlet has the hiccups nobody is safe. There's chaos in the kitchen and disaster at the doctors . . .

CHRIS AND THE DRAGON
Fay Sampson

Chris always seems to be in trouble but he does try extra hard to be good when he is chosen to play Joseph in the school nativity play. This hilarious story ends with a glorious celebration of the Chinese New Year.